Remnant

by
Rebekah Badal

Names: Badal, Rebekah, author.
Title: Remnant / by Rebekah Badal.
Description: New Albany, OH: Rebekah Badal, 2019. | Summary: The Citadel of the tyrant Prince is a dangerous place. A Traveler and a young girl live far away from the Prince's reach, but then they must brave the journey through the Prince's lands to return to the Traveler's home country.
Identifiers: LCCN: 2021923978 | ISBN: 978-1-7329623-2-3 (hardcover) | 978-1-7329623-0-9 (paperback) | 978-1-7329623-1-6 (ebook)
Subjects: LCSH Adventure fiction. | Fantasy fiction. | Christian fiction. | BISAC JUVENILE FICTION / Action & Adventure / General | JUVENILE FICTION / Fantasy & Magic | JUVENILE FICTION / Religious / Christian / General | JUVENILE FICTION / Religious / Christian / Action & Adventure | JUVENILE FICTION / Religious / Christian / Fantasy & Science Fiction
Classification: LCC PZ7.1.B268 Re 2019 | DDC [Fic]--dc23
Printed in the United States of America
First Printing, 2019 Edited by: Connie McVay & Jonica Badal

For business inquiries please send mail to:
P.O. Box 565
New Albany, Ohio 43054

For the Reader

Dear Reader, you are about to embark on a journey from which you will never be the same. This story is written for those who feel lost. For those who need the warm embrace of a father. For those who have never felt unconditional love. Open your heart and mind. Remember what it was like to be an innocent child. But most of all, remember to Trust...

T here once was a man. He was a traveler. The man greatly desired a companion, a friend. For he was lonely. The Traveler searched far and wide. He looked high and low. Every place he went, he searched for an untarnished heart.

But alas! The lands were filled with wickedness. An ancient deception birthed the continuous breeding of darkness. The Prince, the ruler of the land, governed with Violence at his side and Profanity at his feet. Evil reigned in the hearts of his subjects. Not one soul was untouched by the malfeasance of the Prince.

It saddened the Traveler that a companion could not be found. *Who will reject the darkness of the Prince? Who will come with me on my travels?* Was the evil too great? Was the darkness so suffocating? Not one heart held any remnant of light.

One day, the man traveled through one of the cities outside of the Prince's Citadel. The city was built on a mountain top. It was his last stop before returning to his home country. He carried a walking stick and a small bag on his back. These were the few things the Traveler owned. He walked steadily through the dirty streets.

He had a mission, a destiny, but it would not be fulfilled if he did not find a suitable companion. The Traveler's heart was sad and heavy. He'd been searching for a companion for many years.

Loud music playing from inside the brothels drifted into the streets. The torch lights glow cast leering shadows in dark corners. Many people rushed past the Traveler, paying him no mind. Men chasing after women, women chasing after men. Some in rags, others in fine garments. The Traveler walked steadily on. He kept his eyes on the path he traveled.

The Traveler came to the heart of the city, where the richest of the town's men resided. Houses in neat rows lining the streets, became larger and grander as he walked. The people he encountered here were dressed lavishly. Women adorned in fine jewelry, turned their noses up at the Traveler. Men tied their coin purses tighter to their belts, as he walked past them. The Traveler kept his eyes ahead.

Boisterous partygoers, in their drunken stupor, yelled unintelligible vowels from the rooftops of the rich. A large man was thrown out into the dirty street. He landed, splashing into a murky puddle, right in the Traveler's path. Two men had thrown him. Before the men turned away to rejoin the festivities, they spat on the drunkard. The Traveler stopped for a moment and looked down at the soiled man.

"Fancy a good time?" the drunkard stammered as he stood shakily. The man wore clothes that had once been fine but were now dirty and threadbare. "I was growing tired of their turned-up noses anyway. There's a better spot down the way. Come." The man's words were slurred and his gestures slow. He walked on, turned a corner, and did not bother to look back to see if the Traveler had followed.

More people ran past the Traveler, no doubt to find the best parties. The Traveler passed the open courtyard of a rich man. Inside, many were gathered, drinking and eating their fill. Men jeered as a woman, dressed in thin rags, danced drunkenly before them. Her movements haunting, like the music. The Traveler's face was downcast and his heart became heavier and heavier as he walked.

He contemplated giving up his search for a companion. The prospects of finding someone were practically none. This city and its inhabitants proved that with gusto.

Lost in thought, the Traveler almost did not hear the sound above the city clamor and the babel of the parties. A cry. He stopped and looked around. There was a chill in the air as the wind blew. A carriage thundered down the road and the Traveler quickly moved out of the way. He listened, carefully trying to hear the cry again, above the loud voice of the carriage driver. The source of the cry could not be seen.

There. He heard it again. Softer now. The sound was coming from an alleyway. The Traveler sloshed through the muddy street, drawing closer and closer to the sound. Murky water sprayed upward, as he moved, soiling his clothes. He gave not a care. The cry was desperate - a sound of hope, slowing fading.

It was a child's cry. The Traveler found her, hidden away - buried, in a pile of debris. Covered by decaying things. The child lay naked and filthy. Cuts on her tender flesh bled freely. The child's eyes were swollen shut from the many tears shed. Tears left long streaks in the muck that covered her from head to toe. Her little fists were balled up tightly and she was shaking from her uncontrollable sobbing. As the Traveler pulled the babe from the mirth, its breath caught and a soft whining ensued.

The Traveler carried the child out of the city and made camp in the forest outskirts. He took special care in cleaning the child. Tenderly, he washed away the grime covering the child's skin. He disinfected the cuts and scrapes and applied healing salve to soothe the pain, before bandaging her wounds. Bathed and clean, the Traveler clothed the child in warm garments and swaddled her in his own cloak. She did not quiet until the Traveler put the first spoonful of food to her lips. She calmed as her belly became full.

The Traveler smiled. His heart broke for how he had found her- abandoned and alone, dirty from head to toe. No one caring enough to love a small infant. Anger rose in his chest at the thought of the corrupted hearts of the people. The Prince's evil ran deep, severing even the simplest of things- care and love for a child.

As he looked upon the child's innocent face, the Traveler knew he was done searching for a companion. He had found her. A child was an excellent choice!

They would walk many miles together. They would see the great expanses of the earth. He would show her the truth, opening her eyes to great knowledge and understanding. Loving her as simply and as passionately as a little child ought to be loved.

The child grew quickly, only knowing the company and tender love of the Traveler. They stayed far from the raucous cities and the busy towns, tucked away in a cottage hidden in the mountains. The Traveler taught the child's tender heart the difference between the evil of the Prince and the goodness of the Traveler's home country. "What is your home country like?" the child asked the Traveler one day when they were out picking vegetables in their garden.

The Traveler sighed and sat down in the dirt. He wiped his brow before he spoke. The Traveler always took his time when speaking, as if he were thinking about each word carefully before he opened his mouth. "The feeling when you first arrive is like no other. It is like a great weight has been lifted from your soul. The smell of earth freshly coated with dew lightens and cleanses your mind."

The child sat down next to the Traveler. He wrapped his arm around her shoulders and continued. "The beauty of the landscapes puts the Prince's lands to great shame. But it is not the beauty of my home country that makes it great. It is the people who live there and their revered King."

"They have a king?" The child asked thoroughly confused. "Yes," the Traveler replied softly, but his eyes hardened. "But do not for a moment associate the King of my home country with the Prince of these lands."

The child looked up expectantly at the Traveler, waiting for him to continue. "The King and the Prince were once great friends…*brothers*." The

Traveler's eyes were full of sadness as he spoke on. "But their kinship was severed when the Prince betrayed the King."

"What did he do?" the child's voice was small; great was her understanding and innocence. The mere thought of a brother's betrayal made her heart heavy. "I will tell you one day." The Traveler stood from his seat grabbing the basket of vegetables they had picked.

The child stood as well. "Why won't you tell me now?" She whined as they walked back up the stone path to the cottage. The Traveler smiled. "A patient heart is a becoming attribute. Especially in a young one." He stopped walking and turned, bending down to the young girl's level.

"Know this, Young Heart. My words are a promise to you. I will not forget. When I speak, know it is true. Someday will come sooner than you think." And with these words, the Traveler scooped the girl onto his back. She laughed as he trotted back to the cottage, bouncing all the way.

"Where is your home country?" the child asked the Traveler when she lay down in her bed for the night. The Traveler pulled the blankets up to tuck the girl in. "It is a long journey from here. The place it resides is impossible to get to if you veer off course. Once, a long time ago, many knew the path well, but over time those who knew slowly forgot. Others took the knowledge of its existence to the grave. Now, I am the only one who knows the way."

"So, why are you not there now?" The child yawned, her eyelids were heavy with oncoming sleep. The Traveler kissed the child's forehead. "Because I was looking for you.

***

"It is time." The Traveler said one day as the child rose from sleep. "Time for what?" The child looked up at the Traveler with sleep encrusted eyes. "It is time to journey to my home country." The child asked no more questions but simply helped the Traveler pack. "We must pack light and only bring the necessities. The journey will be a rough one."

"Why have we never traveled to your home country before?" The child asked this as she walked alongside the Traveler. Behind them was the cottage and in front of them was the path leading out of the mountains. "You were not ready for such a journey," the Traveler replied, taking the child's small hand in his large, firm grasp.

Making their way down the mountain path was not easy. Stones underfoot and steep inclines caused the child to pause now and then to catch her breath. The Traveler never broke his stride, nor stopped to collect himself.

When the companions made it down the mountain path, the child sat down in the tall grass of the meadow. She needed to rest. The Traveler walked on. "Wait, don't leave me," the child called out. The Traveler stopped and turned around to face her. He smiled. "I will never leave you." He began walking again. "Wait! I need to rest."

The Traveler kept walking. "There is strength still left in you... Come along," the Traveler called out gently. The child stood, her lips poking out in a pout. "There is a stream that runs through the middle of the meadow. We will take rest there." The child dragged her feet but kept following the Traveler.

The child looked around her as they walked through the tall grass. She had never left the comfort of their cottage in the mountains. She had never seen this meadow nor the other towns and villages the Traveler spoke of. Would the places they pass through be as evil as the Traveler said? She wondered if their journey would take them through the city where the Traveler had found her.

The Traveler had told the child many times, the story of the night when he had discovered her as a baby. The child often wondered why, as an infant, she had been thrown into the dirt of the street. Had she cried too much or too loud?

No, that couldn't be. The Traveler never chastised her when she cried. He simply wiped away her tears and told her to be at peace. This always soothed her soul and calmed her spirit. So why had she been cast into the street? The wind whipped around the tall grass of the meadow.

Wildflowers of gold and violet scattered throughout the meadow, looked like the speckles on a nickel bird's wings.

When the companions arrived at the stream, they stopped to rest, just as the Traveler had said they would. They drank the cool, clear water to quench their thirst. There they sat and ate for a time. "What's beyond this meadow?" the girl asked. The Traveler bent down to fill a canteen with fresh stream water. "The meadow goes on for a while, but soon we will come to a small farming town."

"And after that?" The girl sat on a large rock. The canteen dripping wet in his hand, the Traveler stood. He smiled. "One destination at a time. Though we are traveling to my home country, we must still enjoy the journey. I will tell you all you need to know. We will go the way that is best."

The girl scrunched up her eyebrows. The Traveler had not fully answered her question. He put on his pack. "Do you trust me?" The girl looked up at the Traveler from where she sat. Her confusion melted away and she answered from her heart. "Yes."

The Traveler smiled and stretched out his hand. The girl took it and stood. They resumed their journey refreshed. How could the girl not trust the Traveler? He had saved her, raised her, and made her feel safe and loved. She knew nothing else.

***

Many days had passed since the two traveling companions had first set out on their journey. As they went the girl's stamina increased; she grew tired less easily. The weather began to change as they trekked through the meadow. Mild temperatures slowly increased to rising heat. Soft willowy grass became yellowed, dry, and sparse. They had to stop to refresh themselves by the stream more and more often. The stream itself was becoming smaller and murkier as they walked on, until one day it was completely dry.

Underfoot the ground was now cracked and brittle. Tall tufts of sparse dried grass were dotted about the plain. "Do not drink too freely from your water, Young Heart," the Traveler said just as the girl raised her canteen to her parched lips. The girl paused only for a moment before adjusting her intent and taking only a small sip of the cold liquid.

In the far distance, the outlines of the Prince's Citadel stood tall. But nearer still were the farmlands the Traveler had spoken of. The girl's eyes widened. This was not what she had imagined. The farmlands were not green and fertile as she had assumed. The land was barren and dry just like the surrounding landscape.

The Traveler and the girl passed many run-down barns and houses, each in its own state of abandonment. Thick gray dust covered their shoes and made its way inside their soles as they walked. "Where are the people?" the girl asked softly. She didn't need to whisper, but there was something about the stillness of this place that made one feel as though one should.

There was no wind or sound other than the dry ground crunching underfoot. "Not many choose to live here anymore." The Traveler also spoke softly, but his voice was not timid like the girl's. Soon, they came upon a cluster of old structures that looked like they had once been a town center. The buildings were falling apart just like the barns they had seen before. Some spots contained piles of rotting wood and cracked stones where a standing structure had once been. The girl walked closer to the Traveler's side. He took her small hand in his large firm one.

"Do not be afraid. They will not harm you." The girl was confused by the Traveler's words, but only for a moment. It was then that she saw it. A woman, small and skeleton-like. Her hair was hopelessly knotted and her eyes were deeply sunken and dull. Rags hung loosely on her bone-thin frame that stood in the shadows. She was covered from head to foot in the thick gray dust of the barren farmlands. A similar-looking man who was hunched over appeared by her side. The girl felt her heart begin to race, as fear rose in her chest.

Slowly, more skeleton-like figures appeared in and around the broken-down structures of the once town. A father and his two sons stood behind a rotting buckboard wagon. None of them seemed to move at first, but all followed the Traveler and the girl with their unblinking eyes.

"Are they ghosts?" the girl asked as she pressed herself closer to the Traveler.

"No...They are remnants of the past," the Traveler replied. "What happened to them?" The girl was trying not to stare at the father and his two sons, but she could not seem to help herself. "They lost hope..." he explained. The girl looked up at the Traveler. "What do you mean?" She asked.

The Traveler and the girl walked past a young skeleton-like woman who sat on the falling apart steps of a building. "Do you not see it?"

The Traveler's eyes scanned the skeleton-like townspeople. "What is in their hearts is the truth they live in." The girl understood, and the fear in her heart was replaced by a deep sadness. "Can nothing be done for them?" She asked. The Traveler noticed her face had fallen. "Do not pick up what isn't yours, Young Heart. They chose their path long ago."

***

On through the barren farmlands, they journeyed. The nights were cold and the days were hot. Lights from the Citadel shone brighter as the companions drew near. The barren land was vast. It was a far cry from the comforts of their cottage in the mountains. The girl missed their life before this journey.

It seemed like a lifetime ago that she had slept in her warm soft bed. Why was it so important for them to go to the Traveler's home country? Was what they would find there really worth all this trouble? Why couldn't they have stayed in their cottage in the mountains? "Does our journey make you weary, Young Heart?" The Traveler asked suddenly. The girl was startled, but only for a moment. Had the Traveler been listening to her thoughts? "Yes," the girl told the truth. She could never lie to the Traveler. Even the thought of deception was foreign to her heart. "It has been a long time since we slept on something soft or had a warm meal."

A light smile played at the corners of the Traveler's mouth. "We must not light a fire at night. It will attract unwanted guests." The girl looked at the Traveler. "What sort of guests?" The Traveler laughed. "You have a wonderfully curious mind, Young Heart, but it is best that you do not know." The girl poked out her lip as they walked. "I will tell you this, the discomforts are only temporary. Once we get to my home country, we will have all comforts and more than our cottage had to offer."

***

Night fell quickly. The glimmering lights of the Citadel flickered like stars in the distance. The Traveler and the girl were huddled close together under a large withered tree. Sighing deeply, the girl rested her head upon the Traveler's chest. She could hear the steady beat of his heart. It was a comforting sound. One that made her feel ever safe and secure. The girl took a deep breath and the Traveler's scent filled her lungs. He smelled like home. The strong musky smell of pine and the underlining spice of cinnamon coming from him, reminded the girl of the lovely springs days spent in their cottage. Her eyes were heavy with sleep and slowly they began to close.

The Traveler wrapped his arms around the girl and she sunk deeper into his chest. Oh, how deeply the Traveler loved this girl. He wore his heart on his sleeve when it came to her. His chest swelled with deep affection. The greatest joy in his life was to see her smile. He chuckled to himself thinking of their first moments together. And of how the girl as a babe did not stop crying until her belly was full.

The girl felt the rumble in the Traveler's chest. Her eyes opened. "What are you laughing about?" she asked sleepily. "You," the Traveler replied. "Why, what did I do?" the girl yawned. "Nothing, just being you, Young Heart." The girl could hear the Traveler smile. "Get some sleep." He kissed her head.

She closed her eyes, but the girl's mind was still awake. Questions and thoughts swam around in her head. "What is it Young Heart?" the Traveler asked. How did he always know when she had a question for him? "Will you tell me now, the story of how the Prince betrayed the King of your home country?" The Traveler took a few moments before responding. Patiently, the girl waited.

"The Prince and the King were once the truest of brothers. Working side by side, they kept the peace in these lands. Ruling together and subduing all those whose hearts were evil. Until one day the Prince and the King went separate ways. The Prince went to the west and the King to the north.

It was during this separation that the Prince's heart began to change. He began to desire the whole of the lands for himself. Hatred grew steadily in the heart of the Prince. He felt like he was merely the King's lowly servant instead of his equal.

It was at this time that the Prince met some of the most treacherous people of the lands. He let them give him council, feeding his hatred of the King. The Prince's companions were greedy beyond measure. They valued coin above morals. So they devised a plan and presented it to the Prince; they would make him the new king if he would pay the price they asked of him. The Prince's heart was so changed that he paid the hefty sum. With the help of his companions, the Prince established himself as the supreme ruler of the west. Everywhere they went they wreaked havoc and each town succumbed to their power.

The King soon heard word of a Citadel being built in the west. One that was ruled by violence and corruption. Rumor told that the city was being governed by the Prince. The King did not believe this. His own brother ruling a city of filth so vile? He traveled to the city and there he saw the truth for himself. The King was astonished at the level of corruption the Prince had allowed and encouraged. Soon after he entered the Citadel, the King was arrested. He was brought before the Prince and tried on false charges. The King was convicted and banished to the unknown lands beyond the Wall.

The Prince's corruption then spread far and wide with no bounds. It tainted all of the lands that he and the King once kept safe from evil. No one was safe from the Prince's hand."

The Traveler stopped speaking and listened. He heard the soft sounds of the girl's breathing. She had fallen asleep. He kissed her hair and soon he too drifted off.

***

Some days later the girl and the Traveler came to the town just outside of the Citadel. As they drew closer, the girl could see people walking the streets and going about their business. They seemed normal, not like the people of the abandoned town.

The town sat on the edges of a great lake. The lake looked as if it may have once been beautiful, but its waters were now a murky grey color. Bubbles formed here and there on the lake's surface, exploding with wet popping sounds. The lake's sandy shores were littered with the debris of rotting boats and torn fishing nets. The girl only gazed at the disorder from a distance.

It was early morning, but the sun was shrouded over by the thick clouds. A thin fog drifted from the lake and lingered in the streets of the town. The fog swirled around the townspeople's feet as they walked through it. There was something not quite right about this town. The girl's heart began to beat faster. She pressed herself closer to the Traveler. "Do not be anxious, I am here." The sound of the Traveler's voice calmed the girl's rising fear, like cool water on a hot spring day. The girl's heightened breathing slowed at the sound of the Traveler's voice.

The two entered into the bustle of the town. "Stay close by my side, Young Heart. Don't wander off. Though we are not in the Citadel yet, the Prince's hold on this town is strong." The girl looked up at the Traveler. His voice had been firm, but not harsh. She would do as he had said.

As they walked through they passed by many people. The girl studied the people that they passed. Men pushed wheelbarrows full of wilted vegetables or pungent-smelling fish through the streets. Others rode horses or drove carriages through the crossing intersections. Shopkeepers and street vendors either sat or stood near their establishments waiting for customers.

A man carrying a large sack over his shoulder brushed past the girl nearly knocking her to the ground. The Traveler reached out and quickly steadied her. The girl looked up at her assailant. The man looked back at her. His eyes were wide, full of wonder and shock as if he was seeing a ghost. "Are you hurt?" the Traveler asked kneeling to inspect the girl. "No," the girl replied. The man was still staring at her. *Why was he looking at her so intently?*

The Traveler turned his gaze towards the man. The man blinked as if waking from a dream and ran quickly away. "Are you certain you are not hurt?" the Traveler asked turning his attention back to the girl. "Yes, I'm not hurt," she said. They did not begin walking again until the Traveler was satisfied that no harm was done.

They came into a market square where several street vendors were selling their wares. The strange encounter with the man lingered in the girl's thoughts. She wondered why the man had looked at her so strangely. *What was wrong with him?* The girl opened her mouth to ask the Traveler when a particular street vendor caught the girl's eye. There was something odd about the sight of him. At his stand, he was selling jewelry.

Pendants on the cords of necklaces glittered as they swung gently from their hangings. It was not finely made jewelry. But it was made with the care and detail of a craftsman hoping to catch the eye of a lady customer. Suddenly the girl realized what was wrong. There were no women. Every person that they had seen was a man. Another revelation came to the girl's mind. It was not just the strange man who had looked at her so oddly. It was every man they had passed. Each one had looked at her with the same wide-eyed look of wonder and fright. The same look rested in the eyes of this street vendor now.

"Where are the women?" the girl asked the Traveler. "They are gone," he answered softly. The girl looked up at the Traveler. She could see the sadness in his eyes. "What happened to them?" A man guiding a cart-horse crossed in front of the two companions. They stopped to avoid a collision. When the cart horse passed they began walking again and the Traveler spoke. "They were taken by the Prince."

The girl looked back at the street vendor. Handcrafted rings and bracelets with glimmering stones sat in cases propped up to catch the eye of passers-by. But no customers would come to buy this man's jewelry. There were no women to awe at his detailed work. The look in the vendor's eyes now faded as he looked away from the girl. The look of awe was now replaced by emotions of sadness, loss, and hate.

"This was one of the few towns to stand against the Prince after the King was banished. In his rage, the Prince and his men came like pirates in a blood raid and stole away the women. To complete his revenge, the Prince enslaved the women in the Citadel. At his command they do his bidding," the Traveler said. "Why did the men not go and rescue them?" the girl asked. The Traveler took a slow and steady breath. "Look at them closely, then you will see. There are no young able-bodied men left. They are all aged. Too old to fight."

The girl looked at all of the townsmen and saw that what the Traveler said was true. Only old men wandered these streets. "In the Prince's raid, he killed all of the young men. The elders know that if they were to march upon the Citadel, they would all be slaughtered the moment they approached the gate." The girl felt tears begin to form in her eyes. It was not a mystery anymore as to why the men stared at her. She was a reminder of what they had lost and could never recover.

The Traveler looked down at the girl. "Do not be sad Young Heart. Justice will ring true. I assure you, one day the King will take his vengeance on the Prince's wrongdoings." There was something different in the Traveler's voice. As he spoke those last few words, he used a tone the girl had never heard before. The girl looked up at the Traveler. His face held a tightness she had never seen. There was a steeliness in his eyes, his jaw was set. But it melted away just as quickly as she had seen it.

***

The lake town was not very large and as a result, the Traveler and the girl made their exit before sundown. As the two traveling companions began to walk through the town's outskirts, the girl noticed something. The ground beneath her feet was marked like a well-trodden path. "What is it, Young Heart?" the Traveler asked. *How did he always know when something was bothering her?* "The ground is smooth like many have journeyed this way before us."

The fog had dissipated as they left the lake town behind. They could now see properly the landscape before them. Willowy trees and tall grass were painted with the golden light from the setting sun. "Do you doubt the words I spoke to you? About none knowing the way to my home country except I?" The girl's breath caught. She had never once doubted the words of the Traveler. But had she, just for a moment, questioned the truth of his words while observing the path before them? "I-I-," the girl stammered. She did not know what to say.

There was a moment of silence between them. Something uncomfortable pinched the at girl's heart. She had never once questioned the Traveler, never once doubted the truth of his words. Was he angry with her? She dare not look in his eyes for fear of what she might see.

The Traveler stopped walking and knelt before the girl. "Do you trust me?" the Traveler asked, taking her hands in his. His touch was not angry, but gentle. There was a warmth in his voice that compelled the girl to look up at him. His eyes were the same as they always were, full of love and not displeasure. The girl took a deep breath and answered from her heart. "Yes," she said. The girl and the Traveler embraced.

They held each other tightly. This is where the girl felt the safest, wrapped in the Traveler's arms. She had only ever experienced security and love with the Traveler. It was only when they had set out on their journey to his home country when the girl started to experience new feelings of unease and fear. She breathed in deeply and the Traveler's scent filled her lungs. He smelled like home. The strong musky smell of pine and the underlining spice of cinnamon coming from him reminded the girl of the lovely springs days spent in their cottage. The memories filled her with new strength. The journey would soon be over and they would find rest in the Traveler's home country.

"We will be entering the Citadel before the sun rises," the Traveler began. He now held the girl at arm's length looking into her eyes. "We will not be stopping for rest. It is dangerous to spend the night in the city. You must take heart and draw on all your strengths. The Citadel is a treacherous place. Be on your guard." The girl nodded, taking the hand that the Traveler offered.

***

Before long, the path they walked led them to the Citadel gates. The sun had set. It would have been impossible to see in the darkness was it not for the lanterns shining bright all along the walls that enclosed the Citadel. On each side of the gate stood a guard. They looked at the girl and the Traveler with suspicion. The Traveler approached the guards without aversion. "Identification please," said the shortest guard who stood on the right. The Traveler withdrew folded papers from his pocket. "And what is your business in the Citadel?" the shorter guard asked, musing over the papers in his hand. "We seek passage beyond the Wall to my home country."

The guard's eyes went wide at this and he paused for a moment. He looked up at the Traveler and then his eyes wandered to the girl. Across from the first guard was the taller guard, who was also eyeing the girl. The Traveler cleared his throat. The abrupt sound drew the guards' attention back to the Traveler. Locking eyes the guards exchanged subtle nods. The taller guard suddenly left his post and went quickly into the city.

The girl lifted her head and gazed at the enormity of the city. Towers were built high above the Citadel walls. The light from the many lanterns of the city reflected brightly in the girl's eyes. Built on a mountain, the entrance sloped downward and the Citadel's buildings crested higher as one journeyed further in.

Something red caught the girl's eye. She turned and saw a vine-like plant creeping up the side of the city wall. Its tendrils clung tightly to the stone wall it grew under. Scarlet redbuds were sprouting along the vines. One of these buds had blossomed into a beautiful flower. The girl thought it looked like one of the roses that grew in the garden of their cottage up in the mountains. *But no, it wasn't quite a rose. It was different,* the girl thought. The roses they had grown in their garden were smaller and not as rich in color.

The girl moved closer to the bloomed flower to inspect it more closely. The traveler noticed the girl's movement. "Do not pick any of those," he called out. The girl stopped for a moment and nodded faintly. She continued to move towards the vine intending only to get a better look. The flower was unlike any she had ever seen before. The reds of the petals were much richer and the smell so much more fragrant. But underneath the fragrance was an after-scent of something sour. The girl paid no attention to it. So beautiful the bloomed flower was, so overwhelmingly captivating. The Traveler's warning seemed faint and far away now. The girl found herself reaching out to pluck the flower that had caught her eye.

The shorter guard appeared satisfied with the Traveler's papers and handed them back to him. The Traveler turned just as the girl had plucked the ripest of the flowers from the creeping vine. Screaming the girl dropped the flower almost instantly. The Traveler ran to her. Continuing to wail the girl cradled her hand. It was bright red, not just from the blood that dribbled out from where the flower's thorns had pricked her, but red because the skin was burning. The Traveler scooped the girl up as tears streamed from her eyes.

The burning pain in her hand was spreading up to her wrist. Carrying the girl in his arms, they entered the Citadel. The girl could not see the city as her sight was blurred with tears. Why had she not listened to the Traveler? Why had she cast his warning so easily aside? The Traveler sat the girl down on a bench in a corner by a blacksmith's shop. He then went somewhere the girl could not see through her tears. She knew he was nearby and that he would never leave her.

The burning pain continued to creep up her wrist. It was now spreading to her forearm. Her tears increased as she tried to hold back sobs. The Traveler reappeared. In one hand he held a small glass vile and in the other a syringe. He poked the needled through the top of the vile and drew the yellow-colored liquid into the syringe.

The Traveler and the girl's eyes locked. This moment the girl's vision cleared enough that she could see the Traveler's eyes. His eyes were full of pain as if he could feel the burning of the girl's skin within his own. "I need you to be very still, little one," the Traveler said. His voice did not match the emotion in his eyes. Calm was his tone, despite the hurt in his gaze.

The Traveler placed the needle exactly where the flower's thorn had pricked the girl's hand. A few moments passed and the once burning pain that had been creeping up towards the girl's elbow now subsided. It was replaced by a minty cooling sensation that soothed her agony. "I'm sorry," the girl gasped. "I'm sorry," she said again. The words came out choked this time. She felt physically spent and she fell forward into the Traveler's arms. He embraced her tightly and did not say a word. The tears that streamed down the girl's face now were ones of repentance and regret.

How could she not listen to the Traveler? He had never once led her astray. So why had she acted so foolishly now? The Traveler stroked the girl's hair. "Shh, Young Heart do not dwell on the choices of the past. I am not angry with you. The poison no longer runs in your veins. Your blood is pure." Kind and gentle were the words that came from the Traveler's mouth. *He should be angry; he should punish her,* the girl thought. It is, after all exactly what she deserved, but he did not.

"Do not let guilt or shame consume you, Young Heart," the Traveler spoke softly. The girl sniffed. "You asked me once to tell you what the King of my home country is like. I will tell you now." The Traveler pulled away slightly so that he could look into the girl's eyes. His strong arms held her close. "He is the kindest soul you will ever encounter. He is merciful and wise, but most of all, his love knows no bounds. He does not keep a grudge or score of wrongs. The King's very presence fills one with joy and calms the heart with peace. He is my friend."

The Traveler held the girl's face in his hands and gently wiped away her tears. The girl sniffed again. Her heart had calmed and her mind that was once racing with anxious thoughts and fears was now at peace. "He sounds like you," the girl said, softly. The Traveler smiled and was about to laugh when a rough hand grasped his shoulder. The hand tore him away from the girl. "His Imperial Majesty requests to see the man who wishes to go beyond his Wall," said a deep gruff voice, in a mocking tone.

The Traveler looked up at the man who had spoken. It was one of the Prince's soldiers. Three other soldiers had surrounded the Traveler and the girl. Shrugging off the head soldier's grip, the Traveler then extended his hand towards the girl and she took it. The Traveler pulled her close. "Thank you, but we must decline the Prince's request."

The soldiers closed ranks around the Traveler and the girl. "His Majesty's requests are not to be ignored. They are commands to be obeyed," the head soldier said.

Suddenly the girl and the Traveler were wrenched apart by the soldiers. The girl screamed. Two soldiers held the Traveler back, as the head soldier slammed his fist multiple times into the Traveler's face and stomach. The other two soldiers clutched the girl tightly to keep her from running. "Stop it! Stop it! Stop it!" the girl cried. Her pleas were ignored and the head soldier wailed down one last blow that split the Traveler's lip.

The soldiers laughed at their victim's pain. Breathing heavily the Traveler could barely stand on his own feet. His head hung low. The soldiers bound the two traveling companions and began to walk them through the city streets.

The Traveler walked alongside the girl in silence for a long time. Her heart was lodged in her throat at the sight of him. He gave her a reassuring swollen and bloody half-grin. She looked at him with concern. "Do not concern yourself with me, Young Heart," the Traveler whispered. "Everything will be alright. Do you trust me?" The girl answered from her heart. "Yes," she replied as small tears slipped from her eyes. Oh, how the Traveler wished he could wipe away those tears and pull the girl close to him. He wished to comfort her as he so often did before. And oh, how the girl longed for his tender touch. But it was not to be had, because both had their hands bound.

Images of the Citadel came to the girl's eyes, blurred and distorted. The glimpses she had were ones of filth and evil. Pungent smells of vomit and human waste filled her nostrils and made her stomach churn. People, in multi-colored garments, passing by pointed and stared at the Traveler and the girl as if they were a curious spectacle. Others laughed and mocked them; imitating their plight in the most revolting manner before hurrying off to one of the many parties to reenact the story of the imprisoned strangers. *Had the Traveler really taken her away from such a horrid place?* The girl wondered as they drew closer to the Prince's palace.

***

The Prince's Citadel was a deceptive place. It was beautiful and alluring from the outside. Provoking curiosity and suggesting of amusement and thrilling experiences with its twinkling lights. But found on the inside was the exact opposite of the implied adventures. Dirty streets and acrid smells. Citizens with evil in their hearts. Corruption flowing down from the very throne of the Prince, down into the people of the Citadel below.

They all too soon reached the Prince's palace. The gates were opened and the group entered in. The

Traveler and the girl were dragged into a courtyard enclosed by the Wall. On the other side lay the land beyond, where the Traveler's home country awaited. On their right was the gateway, which was closed shut, only to be opened by the Prince's command.

The soldiers shoved the Traveler to his knees on the hard cobblestone of the courtyard. The girl was pushed beside him. She looked at the Traveler, the monster of fear shone in her eyes. "Don't be afraid. I am here," he whispered gently. Blood trickled out from the corner of his mouth. "Do you trust me?" the Traveler whispered. The girl once again looked into the Traveler's eyes. His eyes were calm. There was no fear in them. The girl answered from her heart. "Yes," she whispered.

"They tell me you seek passage beyond my wall to the barren lands," said a smooth voice. The Traveler and the girl looked up. It was the Prince who had spoken. Tall and handsome, he stood at the top of stairs that led down into the courtyard. Behind him was an open doorway into the palace where the sounds of a lively party were underway. The Prince held a drink in his hand, but quickly placed it on the tray of a servant nearby. Dressed in lavish clothing he descended the steps into the courtyard. The Prince's eyes danced with amusement and a light smile played on his lips.

"It is well known that there is nothing beyond my wall but emptiness. So, why then do two of my citizens wish to leave my glorious Citadel?" The Prince came to stand in front of the Traveler and the girl.

"We are returning to my home country," the Traveler replied. The Prince's eyes instantly lost their amusement, becoming steely slits as he peered down at the Traveler.

"You speak blasphemy against my name! There is no country beyond what I have conquered!" the Prince's smooth tone vanished.

"Be that as it may, we still seek passage beyond the Wall," the Traveler said firmly. The girl remained silent. Her trust was in the Traveler.

"Then you know the price that must be paid…" the Prince said slowly as he paced in front of the companions. "A life, for a life…" The Prince's eyes wandered. He looked down at the girl for the first time.

"No!" the Traveler attempted to get to his feet but was pushed down by the soldiers. The Prince looked at the Traveler with a coy smile, as he pulled a dagger from his belt.

"Choose!" the Prince shouted, pointing the sharp blade in the girl's face. She gasped and shrunk away. "The price for passage beyond the wall is a life! Now the question is, who will be the one to go, and who is the one to stay?"

The Traveler was calm. He was unafraid. "The girl must go on," the Traveler simply said, loud enough for the Prince to hear. "I offer my life as payment." The Prince nodded to his soldiers, and they pulled the girl away. Before she could utter a sound in protest, the Prince had raised the dagger and drove the blade straight into the Traveler's heart. His body fell limp on the cobblestone.

"NOOO!" the girl screamed. The sound of her cry echoed in the courtyard. Her vision became blurry as her eyes filled with tears. She could not run to him. She could not stop what was happening. The girl struggled against the soldier's grasp as sounds of pain and sorrow erupted from her mouth. She screamed and wailed. But none of her cries affected the ruthless heart of the Prince. He turned to her. "Your price has been paid in full," the Prince said speaking above her cries. The girl cried out all the more, but nothing would bring back her beloved friend.

"Put her out!" the Prince snapped at his soldiers. The soldiers obeyed their master without question.

"NO!" the girl screamed again as she was carried away. The dead body of the Traveler lay motionless. His life, he had given for the girl's freedom. The Prince turned away from the scene in disgust, walking back to the lively party he had left.

 The gateway opened, and the soldiers threw the girl outside. She landed in the dust as the Wall's only gate closed behind her with an ominous clang. The girl lay still. She couldn't move. She couldn't breathe. A heaviness began to settle deep in her heart. Tears flowed like a raging river from her eyes. The scene of the Traveler's death played over and over in her mind. What would she do now? How could she survive without him?

***

Sometime later the girl opened her eyes. She had fallen asleep in a pool of her own tears. The dimming light of the setting sun filled her eyes. She squinted. The ground around her face had formed into a paste from the tears she had shed. That paste was now dried and clinging to the side of her face. She didn't want to move. Her heart ached. There was a painful hole inside her stomach. The Traveler was dead. Images of his fallen body flashed across the girl's mind. Fresh tears sprang from her eyes and mingled with the dried paste, making it moist again. Her lips trembled. She grieved.

When there were no more tears left to cry, it was then that the girl arose. Before he had died the Traveler had said that she must be the one to go on. *But why,* the girl asked as a fresh wave of sadness came over her.

The sadness was heavy. It threatened to weigh her down. The girl felt like laying back down and staying there forever. But she knew she couldn't. She must finish the journey to the Traveler's home country.

The girl took in her surroundings. Dunes of yellow sand rose all around, stretching for miles in every direction. She could not see the end of them. *Which way must I go?* she wondered as she wiped the again dried paste from her face.

Her heart still aching for her lost companion, the girl set out in the direction of the sunset. The girl's feet dragged as she walked. She was tired and worn. Her emotions drained. The Prince's soldiers had stripped her of all of the supplies that she and the Traveler had packed. She had no food, or water to drink. An unpleasant throbbing settled in the girl's head. Her mouth was dry and her tongue was sticking to the roof of her mouth. She kept walking.

The sun was strange in this sandy place. It did not move. The girl had no sense of time walking among these sand dunes. Hours, minutes, or days might have gone by and the sun stood still. The only sound was the gentle wind kicking sand up off the peaks of the dunes. The girl's tired feet gave way. She fell and her world went black.

***

A lone figure stood on one of the highest sand dunes. The figure watched the girl. He saw her fall and immediately went to her. The girl was unconscious. Her face was dirty and her complexion grey. She felt nothing as someone lifted her from the ground. The lone figure began to walk through the sandy dunes.

For a moment the girl opened her eyes. Her breath was soft and slow. The Traveler was carrying her, just like he often did when she would fall asleep in the tall grass of the garden. He would carry her to her bed. *But that's not possible,* the girl thought. *The Traveler was dead.* Her vision faded to black again.

***

The girl felt herself waking, but she did not want to open her eyes just yet. The blankets that surrounded her were warm and the pillows cradling her head were soft and fluffy. She sank deeper into them and listened for the familiar sound of the Traveler whistling in the garden.

A pain shot to her heart and tears formed in her closed eyes. This was not her bed in the cottage up in the mountains. She would never hear the comforting sound of the Traveler's whistle again. The Traveler was dead.

"Do not be ashamed of your tears child. Weeping is medicine for the soul," said a voice that sounded like cool river waters. The girl opened her eyes and the tears spilled out. She saw a man unlike any she had seen before. Yet there was something familiar in his face that she couldn't quite place. He was large and handsome, but not over-barring. There was a kindness in his eyes, but a fire too. This man was an odd mix of gentle and fierce. The girl knew instantly who he was. It was the King.

She had no words. Only her tears. The King came and sat on the bed next to her, and the girl soon found herself enveloped in his arms. She cried long and loudly for the Traveler; she was missing him with her very soul.

When her wails turned to soft sobs, the girl pulled slowly away from the King to look up at his face. His eyes were watery. He had wept with her. "You were friends," the girl said. "Yes, Young Heart. He was my friend."

The girl was startled. The Traveler had always called her Young Heart. The girl looked closer into the King's eyes. The familiarity the girl had seen finally registered. It was then that she saw him completely and fully for what he truly was. It was like a veil of sunlight had shifted and her eyes had finally adjusted to the light. *It was the Traveler.* The King's appearance had changed slightly to resemble the Traveler. The King was the Traveler. And the Traveler was the King. They were the same man, their beings woven so closely together, yet two different people.

"How…," the girl asked in a breathy voice. It was strange to see the man who raised her, intertwined with the man she had only heard about. "The Prince has forgotten some of the details of the laws in this realm," the Traveler began. "Innocent blood spilled to save the life of another will not be shed without justice. The blameless will awake in the lands of the King because his life was not given in vain. It was given in love. The greatest force in this realm." The Traveler's appearance turned back to the King's but familiar parts of the Traveler remained in his face.

The girl looked at the Traveler-the King, with uncertainty and curiosity. She did not know what to think of him. "I don't think I understand," the girl said. A faint smile appeared on the King's lips. "I will explain it all to you in time, Young Heart." The King reached out and gently wiped away the girl's tears. "Let your tears dry and your heart be lightened. The journey is over. My dear, you are home."

The girl now noticed the room around her. Light streamed in from windows on her right. Outside she could see greenery and what looked like mountains beyond. Carvings riddled wooden double doors that stood ajar. Vines with pink and yellow flowers wrapped around white pillars, that stood tall, around the girl's bed. At the head of the bed, more vines grew on each side, hanging low and trailing from ceiling to floor. A large purple flower hung at eye level on the girl's left. She stared at it for a moment. It reminded her of the flowers that grew on the outside of their cottage in the mountains. Its fragrance smelled like home.

The sunlight coming in the room shifted. The girl looked up and saw the large floor-to-ceiling window on her left. It was not just beautiful, green plants and exotic flowers that met her eyes, a magnificent view of turquoise waters, the ocean. The girl's eyes grew wide and she felt her heart swell. She turned quickly to the King.

"Would you like to go explore?" the King asked. "Yes!" the girl replied excitedly. The King threw his head back and laughed. A deep hearty laugh. When he looked back at the girl, his appearance had returned to resemble the Traveler.

***

The waves of the deep blue waters met the girl's bare feet. She looked at the horizon where the golden sunlight danced on the cresting waves. The King's castle stood on a hill behind them, and towns with cozy cottages full of people lay just beyond.

The King and the girl's hands intertwined as they stood there together. The girl no longer felt sorrow. It was as if a great weight had been lifted from her soul. The smell of earth freshly coated with dew mixed with the scent of seawater; lightened and cleansed her mind. She no longer yearned for her home back in the mountains. She was home. But there was one thing she still did not understand. "What is it, Young Heart?" The King asked, but his voice sounded like the Traveler's. How did he always know when she had a question?

"Will you tell me now, why we had to travel here to your home country?" They were now knee-deep in the water. Another wave lapped at their legs. "When first I set out on my journey through the Prince's lands I went to see if all was as horrid as the rumors had told... It was, and much worse. But I still had hope that there may be one person, one remnant of hope, of goodness left. I traveled throughout the land, looking for goodness, for hope. Then, I found you. The remnant. We journeyed here to my home country to escape the justice to come." The King looked down at the girl. "What do you mean?" she asked.

Turning his gaze out to the horizon, the King explained. "The Prince's days are at their end. I will take vengeance on him for the betrayal of the past. But also for the pollution of the lands. His evil will fall. The lands will be destroyed. And I will restore all to its former glory." Another wave rushed at them. Cries of exotic birds could be heard above the crash of the water, as well as the soft sounds of bells ringing from the towns beyond. "You rescued me." The gentle sea breeze whipped strands of the girl's hair around her face. She now understood. "Yes, Young Heart. For an innocent to befall the justice to come would be a tragedy," the King replied.

The two companions were silent for a time. Each one enjoying the company of the other, as they stared at the beauty around them. The crashing waves, the cry of the birds, and the sun casting its golden light.

Suddenly the King spoke, breaking the silence. "Come, there are many I would like to introduce to you." The girl smiled up at the King and saw the kindness she had always seen in the Traveler's eyes. Before the girl could ask another question, the King splashed her with water.

Blinking the water out of her eyes the girl saw the King run off towards the shore, sloshing through the water as he went. Running after him, the girl splashed water back. He was laughing and the King's appearance changed slightly into the Traveler's, yet he was still the King. They both laughed as they chased each other up and down the sandy beach. The girl's heart never felt so full and rich. She was at home with the Traveler, the King.

The End

Did you enjoy reading this book?

Then please consider sharing your thoughts by writing a review for this title on amazon.com.

OR

Take a picture of the book and share it on social media. Don't forget to tag the author!

Instagram: @bekah_battle

Use the hashtag: #battleprints

Facebook: @Rebekah Badal

Tik-Tok: @hey_bek

When you share or write a review for this book you are helping this title to reach more people.

Thank you!

Acknowledgments

A big thank you to my editors Jonica Badal (mom) and Connie McVay. Without you, this book would never have been published!

To my revival group, thank you for believing in me. I love and miss you all and can't wait for you to read this.

To Jennifer A. Miskov, Ph.D., I say thank you for your wonderful class and book "Writing in the Glory". When I was sitting listening to you speak at the Twin View Bethel Campus, I was inspired. You taught me that writing does not have to be a frustrating process. Just invite Holy Spirit into your writing time and He will do the work.

Thank you to the director of "The Shack" movie. "The Shack" was the inspiration of this book and for that I am grateful.

Thank you to all of my friends who encouraged me during this writing journey.

And last but not least, A MASSIVE THANK YOU to my family. Thank you for your love and support as I chase my dreams and pursue my destiny. Thank you for your faithful prayers and words of encouragement. But most importantly, thank you for believing in who I am and who I am becoming.

About the Author

Rebekah Badal is a graduate of Bethel School of Supernatural Ministry in Redding California. She lives in Ohio with her Mom, Dad, and two older brothers Josh and Elijah. As a child, Rebekah was always an avid reader. This love for reading sparked a passion for writing. Rebekah hopes to write more books in the future and one day even write screenplays.

Follow the Author:

Instagram.com/bekah_battle
Facebook.com/rebekahbadal
Instagram.com/battle_prints

For business inquiries or fan mail please write to:

P.O. Box 565
New Albany, Ohio 43054

www.ingramcontent.com/pod-product-compliance
Lightning Source LLC
Chambersburg PA
CBHW041025170626
46815CB00001B/13